Memento Mori

Simon O'Corra

Bare stage, except for a single armchair and a free-standing swivel mirror.

Lights up on Old Man, sitting, looking into the mirror.

Old Man: There is so much I don't remember. *(looking into a mirror)* I have great memory gaps. No, I am not dementing. Ha! I remember my early years, when times were good, and yet after I reached the age of 25, its all a bit hazy. Obviously, I went through some very hard times, hellish events overtook me then and I only recollect certain parts. WHY? I wish someone could tell me why this has happened.

Young Man: *(entering from behind and placing his hands on the old man's shoulders)* Don't be afraid. I am here and maybe, just maybe, I can help you to find the reason for your patchy memory.

Old Man: Argh it's you? You are back again?

Young Man: Yes, I am. There should be no surprise that I am.

Old Man: I am at a loss as to why you keep returning.

Young Man: Come on now. You are being disingenuous surely.

Old Man: No, I truly do not know.

Young Man: Oh well never mind about why for now.

Old Man: It is good to see you though. Whoever you are.

Young Man: Getting back to your question, why do you think you cannot remember certain aspects of your life?

Old Man: Memories go on for many - its what they do and in a certain sequence. They are a fundamental part of us. But there are gaps and a lack of sequence to mine.

Young Man: Why can't memories be affected too? They are lodged in our cells like everything else we experience. It all makes sense when you think of it.

Old Man: It is troubling though.

Young Man: What is?

Old Man: My memory gaps.

Young Man: What about dementia? That wipes memories doesn't it? Could it be that?

Old Man: No, dementia just disables our ability to access memory. Also, we have the ability to block or compartmentalise bad memories ourselves, but they are still there, they never go away. If you watch some dementing people doing reminiscence work, I mean with music or props, its like the passageways to memories are just blocked up until something sparks them into action for a while. I think the memories remain at the cellular level maybe but what do I know. You know it makes it feel like I have actually been a different person sometimes.

Young Man: Well I think we have, but if we try, we can recapture the experiences of ourselves at different times. I have personal experience of our lives until a certain time of course, but other than that, you should know I have witnessed everything you have done in your life since that time.

Old Man: But I can remember earlier times time easily. How can that be?

Young Man: Well pardon me but some of our shared experiences were shit.

Old Man: The period after the war was not easy believe me. We thought the liberation would make us finally free, but no. The hell carried on, just in a different environment and in a different way.

Young Man: I know nothing of that from direct experience. But because you kept our other memories alive, I have always, as I said before, been around watching your every move.

Old Man: I need to know more about those missing years. Can you help me?

Young man: Why not. Let's go back. I have a story. *(adopting an animated camp attitude)* "I'm not a minor", I told the man on the door.

Old Man: Well not now definitely!

Young Man: You can talk.....

Old Man: I am just saying it the way I see it. Ha! Ha!

Young Man: Anyway, getting back to my story.

Old Man: Oh yes excuse me!

Young Man: He naturally didn't believe me.

Old Man: Well why would he? I remember what you looked like. Rather a late developer.

Young Man: As I was saying! I was in the first flush of youth and really quite feminine as well. He told me I had to be over 30 to get in but I was not, so I couldn't disagree with him about that.

Old Man: That was generous of you and quite proper for you. *(old man laughing)*

Young Man: Bah! *(pause)* He then carried on "The Police will close us down if they see you here.
Come back when you have grown up or grown out of cruising at De Munt or why not try the tea houses? The Maxim is not for you. Go on. On your way." I remember that these names and places were as yet unknown and meant nothing to me. The government had just put up the age of consent for us queers to 21, which meant my twin brother aged 16 was able to fuck his girlfriend, which he did, but if I were to even find a boyfriend, anything we did would be illegal.

Old Man: Hypocrisy will out.

Young Man: Cruising for sex in De Munt was fun and I have always enjoyed a dance. The tea houses were not that bad. The Jazz age was upon us, with all those great dances from America.

Old Man: The Charleston, the Black Bottom, Collegiate Shag were so exciting and like nothing I had seen before.

Young Man: Why don't you dance anymore?

Old Man: *(presenting himself arms outstretched)* You think anyone wants to see this body shaking its shimmy these days? I am also aware of my own physical frailty; I have a weak heart and the spectre of that stays with me always.

Young Man: Just because our bodies change doesn't mean we should not still do the things we loved when we were young.

Old Man: You have no idea.

Young Man: Not at all. You really do have a downer on yourself, think about it. Be rational.

Old Man: Look, I know what my capabilities are now. You don't have an inkling of what it is like to be old.

Young Man: Well no. I am only 28 after all.

Old Man: Such a youth.

Young Man: Of course. Anyway, back to my story. Maxims had opened in 1932 it was the Empire before which had been swish and closed off to a poor people like me. Not long afterwards the place changed its name again to Bob Scheper's 'Bob's-Bar Bodega'. That was where the 'WE' magazine was first started you know.

Old Man: The what?

Young Man: The WE**.** It was a magazine by Johan Ellenberger and his friends who were part of a group called Nederlandsche Vereeniging voor Menschenrecht which was scheduled to be launched there some time later. It was a kind of gay support and activist organisation but the place was closed down by the authorities before its inaugural meeting could be held. The writing was on the wall by that time.

Old Man: Never heard of them. I am amazed you even took the time to know about or remember things like that. I always assumed you were too busy having fun for such lofty ideals. Sex was the order of the day if I remember rightly.

Young Man: Charming. *(pulling a face)* You were the same. Remember? Then in '33' that damn Piront took over at the Bodega and promised the police that gays would not be allowed in from then on.

Old Man: Piront was a shit. Not above selling us all out for profit. Just like the corporations that have taken over our Pride marches these days, they're just in it for the money.

Young Man: This meant none of us common boys or men whatever age could go there anymore. Lucky for some, that Scheper continued to support the more well-heeled gays at his cafe Huize Volendam until the Nazis came to spoil that as well. But this didn't help us much though.

Old Man: *(coming back to a different consciousness)* Yes, I loved those.

Young Man: What do you mean? Love what? What are you talking about? I really worry about you sometimes. Do you mean the dances or the clubs or what?

Old Man: The dances of course. Although I loved the idea of the places too. *(Doing a Charleston badly)* God those were great days, no more restrictions once the War was over. Years later, when we'd grown up, we could live out our fantasies at last and we certainly did. We all needed to forget the wartime troubles. Even though the Great War hadn't touched us directly, it had certainly changed the world's psyche. Nothing was ever the same after that. Whole generations wiped out, well almost. It was horrifying. The first mechanised war, which enabled both sides to kill people *en masse* in just an hour or less. I think that the world suffers in its entirety when a war takes hold of countries and humans kill each other for no rational reason.

People were drunk with relief and even felt guilt for surviving. People suffered from PTSD even though the term had not been invented then.

Young Man: What is that?

Old Man: Shell shock. You know.

Young man: What is that?

Old Man: You are joking? You don' know what shell shock is?

Young Man: Why would I? I was 2 when the War ended. I saw no active service in that war. Ha! HA!

Old Man: Neither did I. Remember?

Young Man: So how do you know so much about it?

Old Man: I am much older than you that's why and have had much more experience of such things. Anyway, at the time it was all hushed up. They couldn't have the masses knowing about this terrible side effect of war. That must by why it passed you by. HA! HA!

Young Man: You really don't like me much do you? So, are you going to explain it to me?

Old Man: Not much point, I think. You are not taking this seriously. Anyway, after the war, soldiers found another way to get over the shell shock they had endured.

Young Man: Oh, go on humour me. I am dying to know more about this shell shock.

Old Man: Alright! The other way they found would appeal to *you* far more anyway.

Young Man: I am all ears.

Old Man: So to get through the horror for men and women was to become hedonistic, and join the crowds of revelers and merry makers. This went on for quite some years despite the Christian's best efforts. We were a strong community, but we were fools. They were just biding their time; they knew where to find us when the time was right. That is exactly what their plan was - to give us free rein. They'd smile and allow us freedoms even as they planned to dismantle our world and destroy us along with it.

Young Man: That is exactly why we must stop being careful and become carefree. If they are going to come for us anyway, why don't we make the most of our lives before they do? They may come for us again sometime so there is no time to sit back and just be grateful for the scraps they deign to feed us.

Old Man: Actually, there was always a grain of shame for me during that time. I was too young to fully appreciate the seriousness and vulnerability of our free status then. I regret that now.

Young Man: You must have hidden that well. I don't remember seeing or feeling shame. It was life and I was grabbing it as best I could.

Old Man: There was no alternative thing to do back then. That is not my experience of life after the war, as things got even worse when I was liberated. I was at death's door and then there was a rumour that we homosexuals would face further punishment, as we had been imprisoned as criminals. I couldn't face all that again, the cruelty and uncertainty. I vowed after liberation I would never risk my safety again.

Young Man: You can be an out gay man now. Why are you still scared and hiding?

Old Man: I am not. The law says I can be out. But if they hadn't changed it, then I would still be hiding myself away.

Young Man: That makes no sense! Let's be honest - you are no longer the banner waving gay you once were. Anyway, you old fool. I don't mean that war! I mean the Great War; you know the one which ended when I was still a baby. When Europe got back to normal at last or so it seemed. It changed everything.

Old Man: That was an exciting time after that war. Part of the thrill was a sense that we were beating the system, albeit with tacit approval of the government. We got to do things that other groups of people didn't, at least for a while.

Young Man: Wake up old man. It's like I don't know you or that you have lost your mind. You think the 'normals' didn't have public sex? If you walked down the streets of 'De Wallen' you'd see plenty of action. A whole spectrum of people all seeking the same thing. Sailors, professors, clerks, stevedores, students. The sex urge knows has no limits. They were all just arse bandits after some young flesh. Do you remember that Catholic Priest, down at De Munt?

Old Man: Who?

Young Man: You know the young priest, the one who used to come in from the country once in a while. He didn't come to increase his flock. He just wanted to relieve himself. Ha! Ha!

Old Man: Ha! HA! I don't know how priests cope with celibacy.

Young Man: That's what we were there for - to service those poor men who had no choice but to obey that archaic church's rules. No wonder they sought us out.

Old Man: Well as so many people use to say "It takes all sorts to make a world"

Young Man: That is right. I remember Bet Van Beeren at Cafe t'Mantje swore by that maxim. She was a truly good person.

Old Man: Yes, I remember her and the Cafe t'Mantje, which was one of the few places we ordinary gays could go without fear of malice or criticism, or murder even. It was great to be safe indoors at last in the mid 30s.

Young Man: A great place full of spirit. Unlike others i have mentioned before.

Old Man: Do you remember Prayer Without End Street and Cripple Alley.? What dives were there, horrendous hovels where anything went, and the shit flowed down the streets. Prayer Without End Street was just so crowded, everyone on top of each other, literally, the barest ray of sunlight piercing the dank courtyards, with prison bar clothes airers at each window, not in the least a bright and airy place to bring up kids, and their were lots of them.

Young Man: Why did all those invalids end up in Cripple Alley?

Old Man: I heard they came there for a cure! There wasn't a sign of God in that passageway though so they must have been hoping for some other kind of relief. Ha! HA! It was even worse than Prayer Without End Street.

Young Man: It was much more obviously Red Light I remember. There were women sitting in windows, young women old before their time, country girls come to Amsterdam seeking a better life, but finding instead an eager pimp ready to exploit them. I bet you wouldn't walk down there, especially if I took you back in time. People got sex where they could, and sex equated to survival for many. Still does in fact.

Old Man: I dare say I wouldn't like those streets now, but I have a vague memory and impression that you didn't mind where we went then.

Young Man: No, we didn't did we?

Old Man: Look where that attitude got us.

Young Man: So, you do acknowledge that you are part of me and I of you? I do know that those cripples were keen for it down there. You wouldn't think they would be but ……..my god they wanted it. Like it was a heightened pleasure for them and their clients.

Old Man: Yes alright. No need to to go on about it.

Young Man: You started it. You can't just open a subject then close it down when the discussion doesn't go the way you want it. What is it with you anyway? So hung up on so many things. Life must be very hard for you.

Old Man: Oh shut up. It's not surprising really, is it?

Young Man: Yes yes you are moaning again I see. You just can't help yourself.

Old Man: No I meant the cripples. They had the least chance of any of us to make a living. They are human after all just like us. Don't you understand that?

Young Man: Hardly, some of them are crooks, out for what they can get. I heard of people who made themselves disabled just to earn some money. I even had a cousin like that and she was a worthless piece of shit. Eugenics had it right back then.

Old Man: You arrogant young bastard, I don't know you sometimes. How can you say that? They were and are human beings like the rest of us. Like you and me.

Young Man: No they're not, anyone can see that. They cannot function as you or I can. They just end up draining the tax guilders that are meant for us who can contribute.

Old Man: BAH! What do you think the camp system was for but a systematic eugenics programme for undesirables? People like us were useless pieces of shit to those bastards in the camps, just the same as any cripple or half-wit was. Or do you think they just treated us that way to get the best out of their workforce? They won both ways. They got the work done and it was an easy way to kill as many of us as possible. God you are stupid sometimes. We homosexuals were on a list of enemies of the Fatherland. We were the 175ers.

Young Man: The what?

Old Man: Homosexuals were punished under a piece of legislation called Paragraph 175 in Germany and to a lesser extent in the Netherlands. They called it something else here. Now what was that again.

Young Man: You are forgetting stuff again old man HA! HA!

Old Man: Go ahead laugh, it comes to something when a homosexual attacks one of his own.

Young Man: Don't be so touchy. Its gay banter that's all.

Old Man: You're cruel. You are just like that law which the Nazis used to encourage the general population into denouncing us.

Young Man: Yeah ok I get it. But at least we could work, although you're right - it was tough, especially for older men. I only just managed to survive it and I was young and look at *me*. I have never regained all the weight I lost. It is funny how one becomes so wedded to suffering so much that you never let yourself trust that you are safe even after the trauma is over.

Old Man: Maybe that is true for me. Perhaps I am not the survivor I think I am.

Young Man: See!

Old Man: You saw what happened when someone was simply too exhausted to work.

Young Man: *(suddenly crying)* You know how to twist the knife.

Old Man: Twist what knife?

Young Man: You know!

Old Man: What?

Young Man: You are so callous. *(wiping away a tear)* I assume you mean Manfred?

Old Man: No, I wasn't talking about him, just in general as well you know. *(looking inside himself for a memory and not finding it, then suddenly)*

Young Man: Convenient that you mention the one truly traumatic episode in our life then. My lover Manfred, the one whose cruel death broke my spirit.

Old Man: No, No don't you dare talk about him, he is mine not yours. You don't deserve him with your louche talk, your ownership of all things gay, a name which didn't even exist then. You make me sick. Don't you dare talk about him.

Young Man: At least I am not afraid of who I am or have been. Anyway, he was mine first and mine completely, more than you will ever know. You cannot even remember him properly or have him in the forefront front of your mind. You are pathetic. You're losing your nerve and your courage. And your mind.

Old Man: Go and fuck yourself. I have decades more experience than you. You know nothing about how I feel. Manfred was my world. He was sweet and gentle.

Young Man: And Lustful and sexy and passionate. Maybe you have projected your own current personality onto him.

Old Man: Don't be stupid!

Young Man: Careful who you are calling stupid. Remember we are the same person fundamentally. Look! Stop! Now we are seeing the true you, the man beneath the veneer of respectability. What use has your experience been? It is not enough to feel, 'being' is what counts. I was with Manfred totally.

Old Man: And I wasn't? It's longer ago but so what? You have no idea about my inner life, the problems I face at my age.

Young Man: Oh boo hoo! Poor you. You, constantly calling me back. What exactly do you think I can do for you?

Old Man: Well clearly nothing! You'll never know I suppose. Stuck as you are back in the war.

Young Man: I'd rather be there than in your shoes now. I can see what has happened in subsequent decades. Look at you. You are a wreck and a shadow of your former self. I don't get why you are so down and worried all the time.

Old Man: Its alright for you. In a sense you are dead and don't have to face this life now. Anyway, seeing is not knowing, it never can be. I have all my own memories and yours too. I lived all those, I am not stuck, just static. It is all I can do to survive now as I am reaching the end of my life.

Young Man: You obviously don't share all our memories. That is what happens when cells die. The fun has gone out of your life. There is nothing joyous anymore because people now, including you, have forgotten the ways in which to live life fully. It ought to be much better now than back in my youth, but assimilation is washing our identities away and it can never mean we are totally safe anyway.

Old Man: Old men's priorities are different to a young man's. Some things are now impossible for me. I can understand you, but I fear you cannot understand me. It is sad that we are so far apart and yet the same person at the heart of ourselves.

Young Man: You admit similarities at last. I think being me really pisses you off. Age is just a convenient excuse with you.

Old Man: Much as it shocks and surprises, me I do. We are not exactly the same though. Experience has fundamentally changed my outlook and age does the rest. You are also stuck in the arrogance of youth - cock sure and defiant.

Young Man: I can say the same about your attitudes now.

Old Man: What do you mean?

Young Man: You haven't cornered the market on being right. You just have a different perception.

Old Man: You make me sick.

Young Man: Careful you could upset some of the others if you are not careful.

Old Man: Don't worry you are the only one I have trouble with.

Young Man: Maybe that is a good sign. Ha! Ha!

Old Man: You are so ill mannered!

Young Man: That is me and I fear, you too. Anyway, we both experienced the sadism of the Nazis. I wasn't so cock sure under them, especially once they found out about our queerness. Every bestial sexual practice was perpetrated by the SS. Unimaginable activities designed to strip us of our dignity and our self-expression. So many rapes and abuses. The human rape was the least of it, if that is remotely possible, I mean the rape with pieces of wood, broom handles, and other things.

Old Man: I know. *(bending double in pain)*

Young Man: In my mind I am stuck in the moment of liberation and before and no wonder. It stopped me in my tracks, and I lost my way and that is because you left me behind. Another period was up, and you had become someone else. A new person. How do you come back from those experiences? How to regain a normal life after that hell. You choose to block them out but we both know you cannot. Age does perplexing things, emotionally, mentally and physically. I remained pretty levelheaded though because I was young.

Old Man: I am not sure you can.

Young Man: Can what?

Old Man: Now who is losing his mind! Regain a normal life.

Young Man: Oh that.

Old Man: You just started a transmutation into another self perhaps, I lost you, you left me or I surged ahead. Me to a new body, new person and new life. I am left with a feeling that I cannot bear to think of those sick times we endured all because of De Munt and the tea houses and the fact I cannot remember those memories that you hold so clearly to quite the same intensity. Why couldn't we stay away from those places? Why couldn't we just get on with our lives and find other ways to be ourselves, It was all so bloody public there. *(pause)* Argh. It was great though. The risk of being caught heightened the pleasure.

Young Man: The tea houses weren't so bad though. Why do you speak so critically of them? I know they were the means by which we came unstuck with the Nazis but they weren't bad in and of themselves. There was a sense of family, real family, unlike the one we had which tied us by blood.

Old Man: Yes, I agree there was a sense we were all in it together despite its shoddy and seedy nature.

Young Man: Anyway, we must think about those hard times. We have to go back there to sort the truth out from the lies. Avoiding them gives them power over us, and life is hard enough without being trapped by emotions. We have to speak to them, write them down, sing them out, scream them from the rooftops, make paintings of them, do whatever it takes to transmute them into positives.

Old Man: It's like pissing in the wind though. The person I was back then has little relevance to me now. Who do I talk to about it all? Who would care about my emotional past?

Young Man: That is irrelevant. The process is about 'you' engaging with it, not necessarily having to confess to anyone else.

Old Man: So you mean I don't have to find a person or a group to share all this with? I can just engage with myself.

Young Man: That's it. So you see maybe I don't need to exist for you after all. But you must remember and talk about those times, it is cathartic no matter how painful. I don't have all the answers, so it has to be you who has to lay them all to rest.

Old Man: Well you are here now with me, so talk……..come on start me off.

Young Man: *(looking beyond the Old Man)* You are such a lazy shit. Must I do everything?

Old Man: Very funny. well the here and now is quite taxing I can tell you.

Young Man: We could start to compare notes on our shared experiences. Share some of the horrors and even some of the good times to temper the angst we both may feel. Why are you complaining? You have such freedoms now old man.

Old Man: 'That's' not a shared experience obviously. We're not off to a good start are we? I am complaining for exactly that reason.

Young Man: What reason? You're not making sense again; I notice this happening more and more with you.

Old Man: So you think I'm losing my mind? Is that what you are saying? No wonder, given what I have been through. You do think I am losing it? It would be no surprise if I were, given the life we have led.

Young Man: We? Careful! Anyway I am sane. Still the vibrant young man I ever was.

Old Man: Yes you died tragically early, only aged 28. You were spared the rest of my life.

Young Man: NO! I have witnessed your subsequent life after I died even though I did not experience it directly.

Old Man: That's the difference.

Young Man: I still just wish you would make sense. Why are you complaining about all the gay rights you have now? Why don't you leave the past where it belongs? Live in the now.

Old Man: I am grateful of course for the theory of it, all the laws I mean, but it feels like it is too late for me. Beatings still happen anyway. These days it seems people are willing to even go to prison just as long as they can kill one us. They think it's worth it.

Young Man: Just look at yourself. I don't recognise you or at least me in you. So leave all that shit behind and just live, why not? If you get bumped off make sure you die happy, having lived a full life.

Old Man: Because as you keep saying I am an 'old man'. I am not an active sexual being these days and all I can look forward to is a care home if I can even find a friendly one. These new laws don't make me feel any safer than I did even before the Nazis came when we were playing with fire.

Young Man: I never felt unsafe. That's you projecting the feelings you have today onto back then. You have it so good now. At least the authorities don't give you hell. It's the prejudiced public you have to watch out for.

Old Man: That is true. I do acknowledge that today of course we do have rights, we 'homosexuals'.

Young Man: Don't use that word. Why do you use that word? I have always hated it.

Old Man: It's what we both grew up with.

Young Man: But you hated it back then.

Old Man: It's what I know. I was mis-treated all my early life because of that word, and it is attached to the horrors we lived through and to what I tried to hold onto in order to survive those terrors. I cannot just forget all that.

Young Man: You can just let it go, you know! You are where you are, so just focus your energy on the here and now.

Old Man: Easier said than done especially as my so-called community no longer sees me as a part of it or even if it sees me at all.

Young Man: You'd be surprised if you only changed your outlook and what you do. You have to get yourself out there. Get yourself heard. You have rights now. That has to count for something.

Old Man: You'll never understand what it is like to age. The so-called community couldn't give a fuck about old me or the vulnerability of ageing, particularly in the late 20th century. Also, laws don't change people's minds and they still seem willing to take the risk of being caught and sent to prison, because for them, one more dead homosexual is job done, even though their life will be shit from then on.

Young Man: Yes you said that before. Don't you remember what it was like to be young and finding a gay life for the very first time?

Old Man: Of course I do. I have not lost my mind completely.

Young Man: You must remember the shadows of De Munt surely, the excitement of it all. I couldn't get into any of the clubs I was just too young and too gay, but those tea houses and those dances and oh those places under the bridge, where anything could happen - they were thrilling times. The joy of it was worth the danger.

Old Man: Now who is repeating himself? I am not sure about that?

Young Man: Whilst you were sucking someone off you didn't think of danger at all. This was what we did then, we had no marriage, no normal stuff, we just found pleasure where we could, away from the gaze of so-called normal people, although quite a lot of them didn't say no to a bit of fun. In fact many came back to the underneath of the bridge again and again.

Old Man: What sad lives those people must have had and all for a quick fuck. They had so much to lose.

Young Man: It was only when I got older that I was able to enter some other secret establishments although they were still watched by the police, but they still carried a frisson of excitement for me and I enjoyed them while it lasted, before I was taken away by the Nazis.

Old Man: Of course I remember such times and the joy they brought. I was there if you hadn't forgotten, but I look back and my memory of the later years is of palpable anxiety which took all my bravery to continue to do those things, for fear of being caught and imprisoned.

Young Man: That is a reflection of how you feel now and not true of that time if I remember correctly. I am closer to those days I suppose. I forget that you were there. HA!

Old Man: You arrogant little shit.

Young Man: I know, it's what allowed me to have such fun back then.

Old Man: Bah! That is unattainable for me now. Those places don't exist in the same way anymore. People are assimilated and that means normalised and conservative except for Pride weekend. Then we become a show and even that is because it is allowed by the mainstream. it's like we are allowed to be truly ourselves once a year. I could not go to such a place now without fearing for my life, I need a safe space to have sex in, if can ever get it and keep it up.

Young Man: HA! We had no trouble back then. HA!

Old Man: No indeed not. It's age darling.

Young Man: Oh Stop It. Age is just a number.

Old Man: Well my number is nearly up. I cannot run so fast now; arthritis is a part of who I am and even the slightest physical violence would definitely do for me. Look at my skin, it's translucent, tissue thin really. Someone could push me over and I'd probably die. So if someone decides he wants to take a gay man out then I am an easy target.

Young Man: Amazing to fear that, considering what we have been through at the hands of those bastards before. They promised work. All those scared people, our neighbours, looking after number one and in fear for their own lives. I can understand it I suppose, but I would never have given anyone up. I was all set to join the Resistance, but the back stabbers got me first. Funny how people hold the wildest grudges. The Act of Denouncing fostered so expertly by the Nazis and NSB was what did for so many of us.

Old Man: We should have known the Nazis made false promises to us. It wasn't an average recruitment policy was it? Herded like cattle, all set to work. How were we supposed to react to that after we had been starved by them in our own homeland?

Young Man: You are right, we had been starved by them in practically every possible way, so it was easy to persuade us with the help of the guns to agree to their demands. It started as a means to take the Jews away, the able-bodied Jewish men, then it wasn't long before they came for us gentiles. Many a bastard took pleasure in settling old scores by accusing us of being in the Resistance or trying to run away, all of that just to save their own skins.

Old man: Sometimes they were just Nazis though, they believed that bullshit. It wasn't just survival but a Supremacist mentality, ideas fostered by the Nazis about minority groups. In a way those who did it for survival were doomed and we knew that. They would face ruin at some point, but the Dutch police, were truly safe to pursue their prey at that time. They took part in the round ups and the denouncing of family and friends. It was your aunt wasn't it that made a career out of denouncing Jews?

Young Man: Yes considering she was a nurse, I was always shocked to know where her prejudice came from. Perhaps it was personal although there was a lot of Anti-Semitic feeling then. God knows why? The Nazis were expert at getting people to do their bidding through personal vendettas. Do you remember Peter?

Old Man: Peter who?

Young Man: Pansy Peter!

Old Man: Oh yes, sweet man, in a hang dog sort of way.

Young Man: He joined the NSB straight away. and really showed his true colours and was a brute once he was in uniform. Weakness! Fear! That is what drives such people to the easy route. Then they feel they have to be doubly cruel to maintain the facade. He would never have treated any of us the way he did unless the government sanctioned it. He didn't have the wit to be that cruel and vindictive.

Old Man: I had no idea, or at least I cannot remember it.

Young Man: He did everything by the book, he never would help anyone. He applied the toughest measures if the rules were infringed.

Old Man: What a shit. Unlike the NSB the Nazis never stopped us from having sex, not before the factories or the camps at least. They were too ignorant, it was easy to deceive them, and their practices at least were not personal.

Young Man: We were pretty much left to our own devices until the Christians started on us and decried our culture of public sex, back in the beginning of the century. They created the perfect environment for hate and disgust.

Old Man: I am with them on that one now.

Young Man: What! I cannot believe after all that has happened you say that now. Aren't you selling out to the mainstream just to get a seat at the banquet? Once you negate who you are you are lost. Respectability can kill a man.

Old Man: No it's just my reality now. I keep telling you. It's different for me now. I am older and there are expectations placed on older people. I pay a heavy price for my misspent youth, as sex for us older men is frowned upon even if it is acknowledged in the first place.

Young Man: Sounds like you are placing boundaries on yourself rather than living who you are. I know you still want the touch a man's flesh under your fingers. I know you still want the ecstasy of two men as one, love mixed with lust, that rapturous feeling when you know the other man wants the same as you. Unspoken just known. But are you saying that you cannot do that now and wouldn't do the same all over again?

Old Man: No,of course not. I was led by my cock and my heart then but now that doesn't matter to me anymore and anyway no one wants an old queen coming onto them.

Young Man: What do you actually remember of those times?

Old Man: It is a long time ago, After the War. No one was stopping us back then, no one was destroying us for who we were born to be. Of course some people didn't like it but the Burgerlijk Wetboek, I mean the constitution, meant it was no one's business but our own as long as we didn't upset anyone.

Young Man: Which war?

Old Man: The first one. The one we were not involved in.

Young Man: Oh I see, it certainly changed everything, that one.

Old Man: Yes , so you see, we did have some freedom back then.

Young Man: Exactly. We were free to be ourselves and there were many places which catered for our needs. Remember?

Old Man: Yes I said so didn't I?

Young Man: Well not in so many words no. We ought to share our experiences and see if they match up. We surely must remember the same things even if we differ in how we feel about them now.

Old Man: You think they will? Maybe you have something there. Maybe how I have felt over the years has coloured my ability to remember things. We haven't even talked about the camps yet. I find it both hard and easy to remember that time. Perhaps it is the extremes that make this difficult.

Young Man: Well they ought to at least match somewhere, somehow after all we are……

Old Man: I know I know they should.

Young Man: How do you know?

Old Man: Talking to you is making me realise. Back in the heady days of love and joy and sex, we thought they were not looking, but they were, and just waiting for the time to pay us back. Now with this pained body I cannot run away I am easy prey. So you see I cannot go to the places we used to go and I cannot do things we used to do. I sometimes have the desire but zero ability. Everything is a struggle now and I prefer not to put myself harm's way.

Young Man: I didn't get taken during the Round-ups because I fucked men, I was just unfortunate enough to be young and they needed all able bodied, strong and young men for their factories in Germany, even though I was not Jewish, which was what they wanted to start with. It was expedient to use us Gentiles eventually.

Old Man: But making love to men got you into trouble later.

Young Man: Yes of course but I wasn't making love then, that came later.

Old Man: During your time in the camps I suppose.

Young Man: Don't be a fool. I couldn't wait for years for sex or love. Who could?

Old Man: After liberation I just waited and waited and waited, in fact I'm still waiting, oh not for sex that was never in short supply until twenty years ago, but love? That is another question entirely.

Young Man: Once I found love everything changed for me, in the camp I mean. The camp was very hard but it had its attractions and the warmth of a lover overcame anything.

Old Man: Attractions? What on earth could you find to attract you in those hell holes? I just lived moment to moment focusing on survival. The clay pits were horrible.

Young Man: No you mean the quarry.

Old Man: No the clay pits. I know what I am talking about.

Young Man: There was no clay pit at Mathausen. Mathausen was the camp of stone not clay.

Old Man: This is weird. Alright so you tell me about Mathausen.

Young Man: You must know about Mathausen.

Old Man: I don't at all. I told you.

Young Man: But you remember Manfred?

Old Man: Yes of course.

Young Man: He was at Mathausen.

Old Man: No he cannot have been. He was at the factory.

Young Man: No he was at Mathausen.

Old Man: NO

Young Man: Let me tell, you about Mathausen and see if you can remember a little of what went on there.

Old Man: Alright. But I cannot remember it at all and I am sure Manfred was at the factory in Berlin.

Young Man: We struggled with those damn back-carriers endlessly. Someone made reference to us being like

Tyrolean peasants, but they were not part of some pastoral scene believe me. Those fucking things broke our backs in more than one way, first of course the sheer weight was indescribable but because they were constructed of wooden planks there was no arc in their construction to follow the shape of a man's spine. *(Old man feels a pain in his back)* The middle of your spine felt the weight with no physical contact to soften the blow. Those leather straps too with weeks and months of mud were rock hard and cut into our shoulders terribly. You couldn't even choose to take a smaller stone as if the SS or Kapos saw you they would, after the trial of the steps and the steep climb, persuade fellow prisoners to push you over the edge of the cliff to your death.

Old Man: That sounds horrific. I still cannot remember Mathausen. What came after sticks in my mind more. I suppose I simply may have chosen to remember one of these experiences rather than both. Tell me about the steps?

Young Man: The steps were cut out of the clay and the rock and had wooden planks to support their construction. This made those fucking steps lethal slippery death traps in themselves, never mind having to haul large pieces of granite up and sometimes down them.

Old Man: Why would you bring the stones back down to the quarry bed? That's stupid having just carried them up to waiting trucks.

Young Man: The SS were bastards like that. They used to taunt us with these crazy demands just because they could. That is how they broke the spirits of most of us there. Can you imagine having made a supreme effort to get a block of stone up the steps perhaps for the tenth time that day and then as you got to the top for the last time and could feel the end of the working day upon you, they would send you down and of course get you to bring that fucking granite block back up again.

Old Man: Funny I just do not remember that.

Young Man: How can that be?

Old Man: I suppose it may be to do with the change that came towards the end of that experience, when you left me I mean, when the cells died off again. Perhaps that leaving allowed me to divest some hideous memories.

Young Man: What the fuck are you talking about?

Old Man: Well there is the theory that all our cells renew themselves at seven to ten year intervals and I know for me, that major life cycles have occurred roughly every seven years.

Young Man: That is mad.

Old Man: Is it?

Young Man: That would mean I am non-existent. I cannot believe that.

Old Man: It would explain how at a terrifying time in our shared life we have different memories because we were and are fundamentally different people.

Young Man: Funny but I cannot remember personal and experiential memories beyond my death just after the war at Mathausen. I died in there just after liberation.

Old Man: No! You died in 1944. This was the end of the 4th cycle and that was the year I was moved.

Young Man: Oh I see what you are saying now. Maybe because when all our cells from seven years back died, in 1944. I was no longer able to experience your, sorry our life, afterwards, but simply was able just to witness things from afar, becoming a kind of ghost.

Old Man: Mathausen was before I was moved away to another place. Surely you must remember Neuengamme? At least as a witness.

Young Man: Where?

Old Man: Neuengamme Camp, the clay pit. The brickworks. The river banks. A torment.

Young Man: I was never there! Never heard of it even.

Old Man: That must have been the time then.

Young Man: Time for what?

Old Man: As I said before when you left me! When our accumulated cells of the last seven years finally died off and I was transmuted into a new entity, not at least the me that you see now.

Young Man: This is stupid. No I was there at the end of the war. I remember the liberation.

Old Man: You can't! Your withdrawal must be what you remember as a kind of liberation. No I was obviously moved after Mathausen I remember that now, the immense relief I felt. *(suddenly stretching)* I didn't miss those back-breaking stones I can tell you. Your war ended sometime during your time at Mathausen, that's when you lost me. That must be it.

Young Man: Lost you?

Old Man: As we have said when the cells that were you finally died off.

Young Man: Oh I see *(looking dejected and betrayed)*

Old Man: Neuengamme was a hell hole. I never since have I seen so much mud mixed with blood. I was spared the the hard work and the beatings as my task there was clerical. had developed skills in office work in the factory in Berlin. I was transferred because I had this experience and also in supplies. I was crucial to keep the camp's work going.

Young Man: You came up in the world, you reached new heights without me.

Old Man: Don't be bitter.

Young Man: I am not bitter more like pissed off. I could have done with a break from Mathausen's worst excesses.

Old Man: The guards at Neuengamme were always ready to beat the prisoners. They worked them from morning to night, regardless of whether it was raining, hot, or freezing, sometimes enough to be frostbitten. They were all forced to work 10 to 12 hours a day, without enough food and hardly any clothing.

Young Man: You did alright though.

Old Man: I was very lucky I have to say, all thanks to an SS man at my previous place which must have been Mathausen. I was my block Kapo's bitch but an SS man there desired me too and was prepared to do whatever it took to get me. This was a massive risk for him and even more so for me.

Young Man: So you did have some courage back then.

Old Man: He got me out because by chance he discovered that my old lover the Kapo was stealing from the SS kitchens or so it seemed. A serious crime. So the Kapo had to give me up if he wanted to live. The relationship with the SS man didn't last long though, in a sense it was doomed for all concerned. Another Kapo threatened to betray the SS man and I was removed before it all blew up and reached the ears of the Kommandant. He must have had something really serious on the officer, I never heard of another SS man being so publicly denounced. He was sent to the Eastern Front. I never heard of him afterwards.

Young Man: I am seeing you in a new light.

Old Man: Hardly. I thought you had still witnessed everything in my life even though you had left me.

Young Man: Funny! HA! HA!

Old Man: Anyway enough of that**.** Back to Neuengamme. I saw men dying from overwork, often caused by blood poisoning from the beatings and the filth, or from pneumonia and other diseases. The Nazis' aim as always was to extract the most work out of inmates and simply after that oversee their death either by killing, abusing, neglecting or starving them. The SS and their Kapos wanted the pace always to be fast and they were there with their clubs ready to encourage everyone to maintain the rate of work. When people could work no more, they often fell to the ground lifeless and the SS and the Kapos would still beat them until they moved no longer either because they had become unconscious or were actually dead. After a long hard day the remaining prisoners still had to carry between 20 and 30 prisoners in these states back to the camp for roll call. Everyone had to be accounted for at evening roll-call, dead or alive.

Young Man: I suppose you wrote down the names at roll call too.

Old Man: No of course not. That wasn't my job.

Young Man: It is no different to Mathausen but I guess you could stand back from the privations in your new role. If you were there in this new place at all.

Old Man: I am not lying. This is what happened to me after you had gone. Anyway, I at least was able to bear witness to the horrors perpetrated there and survived to tell the tale.

Young Man: It is hard to believe. You are saying you were there in Mathausen and now you are saying you were also at Neuengamme. This is horrifying.

Old Man: As I said I have blocked the memories from Mathausen except Manfred of course.

Young Man: So you believe me about Manfred after all?

Old Man: Well it seems plausible especially as you are a younger me. You should know I suppose.

Young Man: I still don't understand how did you not grow from this experience. Look at you now you silly old fool. There seems nothing much to show for all that effort, all that pain.

Old Man: What do you mean?

Young Man: Where have you gone? You are back in the closet, to all intents and purposes.

Old Man: No I'm not, I am still here. I am out as you call it in my own way. I have more of this story if you want to carry on hearing it.

Young Man: You think so? I cannot see you are but do go ahead with the story.

Old Man: That's a wicked thing to say. Why are you so cruel?

Young Man: True though. We wouldn't be arguing otherwise, it proves my point. I don't recognise you, not because in the natural order of things you have changed with age and experience, but that in fact, you have totally changed, so to me you are a different person entirely.

Old Man: You are just provoking me now. Why do you feel you have to do that. My life cannot impact on yours. What I do now is nothing to do with you.

Young Man: Why would I bother doing that? You are just alien to me now. Yes you're right, nothing you do impacts on me, just makes me sad a little. I guess if it makes you feel better carry on with the story.

Old Man: Well just before liberation, thousands of the Neuengamme prisoners were marched off to the coast and forced to board ships to take them away. I wanted to be part of that march I can tell you. Once the people were on board, excited to be leaving the mainland, the Allies, then mistaking the ships for those carrying cowardly fleeing Nazis to Norway, bombed all four ships killing most of the occupants. Those surviving were mostly shot by the Nazis as they swam ashore. Out of around 9000 only 450 survived.

Young Man: So you survived that carnage? That was lucky. Landed on your feet again eh!

Old Man: No silly I was not there.

Young Man: Where were you then? Had you escaped already?

Old Man: No I was back at Neuengamme, one of 6 or 7 hundred of us inmates, charged with cleansing the camp and most importantly, destroying vital evidence of the Nazi's crimes. This was the most sickening task of all for me, enabling the Nazis to exonerate themselves from responsibility for so much horror and murder.

Young Man: You did survive though?

Old Man: Well obviously. The Soviets were first there to liberate the camp, but they didn't treat us pink triangle prisoners very well. We faced more abuse and sometimes sexual attacks and beatings. Then the British arrived and things got better. I began to have hope that all would be well.

Young Man: So did you go home? Wait a minute! Why am I asking you questions when I ought to know the answers? I have witnessed other aspects of your life post ME. Why cannot I remember what happened next?

Old Man: I think that when an entity dies, like you did, then the years immediately afterwards are hidden from you. You said you didn't know anything about Neuengamme, so there is no reason to assume that you would have recall of what happened to me in Post War life.

Young Man: Possibly yes. Go on then, tell me more.

Old Man: I did go home yes, and that should have signified the end but still the Dutch Police had it in for many of us returning asocials. They had been in charge of the running of the Netherlands and many were able to keep their jobs despite having committed atrocities.

Young Man: What shits! How did they manage to go unpunished?

Old Man: Well, as I say, many had specialist skills and knowledge, and others were 'persuasive' , like your aunt, the nurse. Anyway, a few months after my return, the police came for me and charged with me indecency. I was committed for trial and then sentenced to some time in prison. After all I had gone through, suddenly I found myself on the wrong side of the law again.

Young Man: I can imagine that was hell, but why are you like this *(looking him up and down)* now.

Old Man: You mean why am I downtrodden I suppose? You just don't understand what its like now. A new Millennium is upon us but are things really much different to back then?

Young Man: Of course I understand how you are now, but I also see the world that you gays inhabit. All looks pretty good to me.

Old Man: We homosexuals don't have it as easy as you think.

Young Man: Why can't you be gay?

Old Man: I love me. What more do you need to know?

Young Man: Go on say it. 'GAY'.

Old Man: No it's not how I identify myself.

Young Man: But it's who you are. It's who we have always been. You can call it queer if you prefer.

Old Man: That's even worse. I'm not queer. Loving men is only part of me. I am quite normal in other things.

Young Man: Oh you're queer dear, believe me! You just don't know it.

Old Man: I am not camp, I don't do drag, I am strong even for my age, although still weak in real terms, but that doesn't make me queer or gay. I don't know how I can possibly be queer?

Young Man: You are supposed to be the older, you have seen and experienced more life than I have. You buried me remember?

Old Man: Buried you? You make it sound like a willful act on my behalf.

Young Man: Sure, you grew down or got smaller I think and closed off parts of you that related to me. I am amazed that we are having this conversation even. It is very interesting to me why now, of all times, you choose to engage with me.

Old Man: I just changed, we all do, as we have discussed. Every 7 years we are a completely different person at a cellular level. So you think I called you in now? You are decades away from me. So we have even less in common.

Young Man: Well someone did. I would never impose myself on anyone without being asked first. Well that isn't exactly true, in a sexual sense when I stop to think about it. Do you remember Vincent? He was a God and ultimately got us into trouble.

Old Man: I do remember him yes. We cannot blame him though. He didn't ask to be so beautiful but he could have been more careful. He was like you, full of himself and sure of his desires and totally without fear.

Young Man: Yes and look at YOU now. What happened to you?

Old Man: I told you before, you can never know what it is like to be me now.

Young Man: You talk as though we are different people.

Old Man: We are, as are the times we live in. Lets be clear - it is not easy these days.

Young Man: So I don't count anymore?

Old Man: Well in a sense you no longer exist, you are a part of me that is not actually tangible.

Young Man: I'm not tangible?

Old Man: You may just be me holding forth trying to relive some of my glorious and terrifying past.

Young Man: You're deluded. I am saying it the way it was and is now. You've lost it man.

Old Man: There was a certainty in the factory and in the camps. You knew where you were. The life was proscribed and the worst that could happen to you was death which haunted you every day anyway.

Young Man: There is no doubting that, but what has that to do with who I am in the here and now?

Old Man: BAH!!! *(pause)* Now I find I can be happy, life as it is lived today allows some happiness and contentment and some pride in oneself. But…………

Young Man: You don't sound proud to me. You sound scared. Even in the camps I had a relationship. I found love greater than the lust I had known before. But. What have you now?

Old Man: I have vulnerability occasioned by age and a changing tide of homophobia, is that what it is called? And It is all mixed in with a legal right to be who I am which is so confusing after all we have been through.

Young Man: That is all in your head man. Even without laws, you can be who you are, if you choose to. You do not need them to be you a fully out gay man.

Old Man: Believe me I am in no way gay, not in the old sense of the word anyway. I am sad, full of regret and fear.

Young Man: You cannot be more scared than we were in Mauthausen and you were in Neuengamme.

Old Man: We don't have the market cornered in fear just because we experienced the Holocaust. There are different kinds of fear and to build a hierarchy of oppression sets us victims against each other, like now.

Young Man: I am not a victim. I came through a difficult situation. I am not against you dear man. I am simply trying to understand how you have lost touch with me and who we were so completely.

Old Man: It is inevitable we lose touch with ourselves and any attempt to hold on to our old selves is pure artifice.

Young Man: But in our core is a collective consciousness, memories and soul pathways.

Old Man: You believe that?

Young Man: Of course. If not, then how do you remember me and what we used to do?

Old Man: Fair point I suppose. It may not work the other way though. We are not the same person now as we, I mean you, were back then. Fifty years have passed, and I have no single cell in my body now that was around in you in the 1940s.

Young Man: But what about the inside of these cells?

Old Man: You mean the DNA I suppose? Well yes I suppose they keep us the same to an extent.

Young Man: But how. What is it that is still around?

Old Man: Our soul maybe?

Young Man: I thought you pooh-poohed all that soul stuff. Don't get all religious on me now. I had enough of that from my father.

Old Man: I cannot remember him really. He is a part of my life that was before the horror.

Young Man: But I can see him, smell him, hear him as clear as the day I last saw him.

Old Man: He wasn't against who we were/are? At least I don't think so.

Young Man: What! You don't remember? He was not happy at all, afraid of the neighbours and those who might denounce him to the Nazis for having a gay son. That was true of many people back then, afraid of their own shadows. He would much rather sell me out to them rather than protect me and risk his own life. Denouncement became a way to settle old scores, even within families. Surely not people say, but so many people betrayed their families as a convenient way to protect themselves.

Old Man: He would never have done that surely?

Young Man: No but he pushed me in the direction of the Round-ups instead.

Old Man: Maybe that was an act of love though. You survived in the camps until your cellular time was up.

Young Man: Is that supposed to make me feel better? I wonder about you sometimes I really do. Where has all your fight gone?

Old Man: Why can't you turn it around and have it be a kind and generous thing he did. He was a kind father when we were very young.

Young Man: Don't you remember that night when he told me/you that I had better give myself up to them because I would at least be earning money? Little did he know that he was so wrong. We may have been relatively safe, but we were slave labour that is all.

Old Man: No, I don't remember that. My first memory is a letter I got from him at the German factory. He said he was proud of me. That meant the world to me, didn't it to you? His pride in me got me through the worst of what was to come.

Young Man: And why was he proud? Proud of what do you think?

Old Man: That I was working and that I was safe and the rest of the family were safe too. He did the very best to love us. I don't now why you mis-judge him so.

Young Man: There you have it. That is the real reason he was grateful and proud.

Old Man: What do you mean? You're not making sense.

Young Man: Your wicked lifestyle was away from him and not going to cause him or the family any trouble. Didn't you even look beyond his words and never feel marginalised by his pride? I wonder your memory isn't manufactured anyway to help you through the worst of your experiences.

Old Man: I was just happy he was proud of me, which in a way made it easier to be who I was, because I was not going to cause him any trouble from then on.

Young Man: You are lying to yourself and others though if you are not totally out to everyone. Still, you don't want to rock the boat do you? Even now. It's who you are - the peacemaker. You'd rather sacrifice who you could be rather than be who you really, in fact, are.

Old Man: You never were.

Young Man: No not a peacemaker, never. Why should I be? I had as much right as anyone to be myself.

Old Man: Not at a cost to anyone else though.

Young Man: We all must live our lives as we see fit. There would be much less trouble in the world if this was applied by everyone.

Old Man: That's just too easy for you to say. There is always a cost. We cannot keep causing pain and suffering because we want to express ourselves to the detriment of others.

Young Man: Assimilation again talking. How come that doesn't apply to our father? If we all respect each other despite our feelings, then we can all just get on. Its better than giving in to another's self-satisfied bigotry. His self-preservation cost us dearly, Why do you blame me and not him?

Old Man: It was the Nazis who took us away not him who sent us. I cannot believe that of him.

Young Man: But our neighbours and sometimes our families betrayed us for their own purposes. The Nazis may not have gotten us if they had not betrayed us.

Old Man: But to blame them when they were in a system not of their making is unfair.

Young Man: So did they not have any choice?

Old Man: Of course not, unless they wanted to join the Resistance and live rough for years, under fed, with no security and under a constant threat of death.

Young Man: So they did have a choice then after all.

Old Man: Not really a choice. You have to be a certain kind of person to stand up like that.

Young Man: Yes that is called integrity and humanity. You are now hiding your sexuality again for fear of what exactly?

Old Man: That is unfair.

Young Man: So you do acknowledge that some people can be unfair? Just the ones who have no power.

Old Man: What are you talking about?

Young Man: You feel you can blame the Nazis and now me, but not the unfair treatment that our father gave out. That was ok because he had no choice.

Old Man: Pah!

Young Man: You just don't get it. You are just like him and our neighbours, morally weak.

Old Man: What do you mean? I told you it is what comes with age, weakness I mean. My body doesn't do what it used to.

Young Man: I don't mean your physical self. Unless you count your lack of backbone.

Old Man: Now that is unfair. You and I are cut from the same cloth. If I am weak then so are you.

Young Man: Oh no. We may have the same conception point and even some shared history, but we are as different as any two people could be in all ways. Anyway, I survived.

Old Man: Yes for as long as it suited you. Then you disappeared. You were, to all intents and purposes, dead to me.

Young Man: That is rather the wrong way of looking at it. It was you who shed me, not the other way around. Of course, I am dead in reality. It was you who made me die.

Old Man: Is that why you come back to haunt me?

Young Man: Don't flatter yourself, I am not haunting you. I'm fact it is quite the opposite with your constant looking back and refusing to change in the now. You are haunting me by your obsessive recall, in an effort to make your current life better. You have to live as best you can in the now. If you don't look back then all is the present and a glorious unencumbered future.

Old Man: I didn't call for you. How could I?

Young Man: By dreaming of a better time and a desire to make your current life resemble your past life, in its all its horrors.

Old Man: You appeared to me though.

Young Man: So you don't, like in so many other ways, take responsibility for that? We have to stop this. We have reached the end I think. We have different views of our life and I suppose we always will have.

Old Man: Listen I am too tired to keep you here. We've said it all now haven't we? We'll have to agree to differ. I need to rest now and find some peace before it is too late. These things I experienced have gotten the better of me over the years. I now realise only death will truly liberate me. The Nazis have been winning all this time, despite them not being around anymore, well at least not in their old guise. Now though, the storm is coming once again and I must release you now before it is too late for us both. *(slumping in his chair)*

Young Man: You release me? What do you mean? This is the last time you shall have the pleasure of my company. I need to leave now and as for you, you are going to become just a memory now as I have been for you, like some entry in an old Nazi register with no one to recall you back, as you have me. Now I'll be at peace too thankfully. I am leaving now old man. *(beginning to walk into the darkness).*

Old Man: You know I thank you for being with me and in fact for being me at one time. I am sorry for dragging you back here to mull over these days of ours and those of mine you cannot know. *(looking in the mirror again)* I am coming to the end of this cellular life and must face my true end. There will be no other entity after me. I am the last in a line of life forms bearing my name. You are right. I will be snuffed out but with no one to come back for, no one to help in understanding how life works and what it is all for, and no one to pester with all these damn questions you have been asking me. I thank you for the opportunity to ask you the questions that I needed answering. You are lucky you had both.

Young Man: Both? Thanking me for what? You are not making sense old man. Just fuck off. *(leaving)*

Old Man: Questions and Answers. *(waving the Young Man away)* Farewell, go in peace dear man and thank you.

(The Young Man exits, the old man slumps in his chair. LIGHTS OUT)

www.ingramcontent.com/pod-product-compliance
Ingram Content Group UK Ltd.
Pitfield, Milton Keynes, MK11 3LW, UK
UKHW021528300726
14060UKWH00011B/23

9 780244 506889